P9-AOE-150

Dear Parent:

Buckle up! You are about to join your child on a very exciting journey. The destination? Independent reading!

Road to Reading will help you and your child get there. The program offers books at five levels, or Miles, that accompany children from their first attempts at reading to successfully reading on their own. Each Mile is paved with engaging stories and delightful artwork.

Getting Started
For children who know the alphabet and are eager to begin reading
• easy words • fun rhythms • big type • picture clues

Reading With Help
For children who recognize some words and sound out others with help
• short sentences • pattern stories • simple plotlines

Reading On Your Own
For children who are ready to read easy stories by themselves
• longer sentences • more complex plotlines • easy dialogue

First Chapter Books
For children who want to take the plunge into chapter books
• bite-size chapters • short paragraphs • full-color art

Chapter Books
For children who are comfortable reading independently
• longer chapters • occasional black-and-white illustrations

There's no need to hurry through the Miles. Road to Reading is designed without age or grade levels. Children can progress at their own speed, developing confidence and pride in their reading ability no matter what their age or grade.

So sit back and enjoy the ride—every Mile of the way!

For Artemis,
and for Sarah Rose Rothenberg
on her Bat Mitzvah
"Clever, brave, and beautiful"
C.D.

To Anita, with many thanks
A.N.

Library of Congress Cataloging-in-Publication Data
Demas, Corinne.
The magic apple / by Corinne Demas ; illustrated by Alexi Natchev.
   p.   cm. — (Road to reading, mile 3)
Summary: In their travels, three sisters find a magic spyglass, a magic horse, and a
magic apple, which they use to help save a sick prince.
ISBN 0-307-26334-7 (pbk) — ISBN 0-307-46334-6 (GB)
[1. Jews—Folklore. 2. Folklore.] I. Natchev, Alexi, ill. II. Title. III. Series.
PZ8.1.D373 Mag 2001
398.2'089'924—dc21   00-064669

A GOLDEN BOOK • **New York**
Golden Books Publishing Company, Inc. New York, New York 10106

ISBN: 0-307-26334-7 (pbk)
ISBN: 0-307-46334-6 (GB)

10 9 8 7 6 5 4 3 2 1

The Magic Apple

by Corinne Demas

illustrated by Alexi Natchev

Once there were three sisters
who were clever, brave,
and beautiful.
Ella was the oldest sister.
Bella was the middle sister.
And Stella was the youngest sister.

They all loved to journey
far and wide
in search of adventure.

One day, the oldest sister, Ella,
traveled to a faraway city
by the sea.
There, she met a sailor
with a spyglass for sale.
Through it she could see
distant ships as if they were
right up close.

"I'll buy this to show my sisters,"
she said.
But the spyglass cost
every penny she had.

"It's a magic spyglass,"
    the sailor told her.
"Turn the knob
    and you can see things
    on the other side of the world."

"My sisters will love this,"
said Ella.
She bought the spyglass
and headed back home.

The middle sister, Bella,

traveled to a faraway mountain.

There, she met a stable hand

with a horse for sale.

The horse was big and very fast.

"I'll buy him,
   and my sisters and I
   can all ride him together,"
she said.
But the horse cost
   every penny she had.

"It's a magic horse,"
  the stable hand told her.
"He can take you to
  the other side of the world.
Just whisper in his ear
  where you want to go."

Bella bought the horse.
She climbed on his back
and whispered in his ear.
In a flash, she was back home.

The youngest sister, Stella,
traveled to a faraway valley.

There, she met a farmer
tending an orchard of peach trees.

On one tree,
among all the peaches,
grew a single apple.
The apple was the largest,
reddest, most perfect apple
Stella had ever seen.

"I'll buy this apple to show
my sisters," said Stella.
But the apple cost
every penny she had.

"It's a magic apple,"
the farmer told her.
"It will bring you good fortune."
Stella asked what he meant,
but he would say nothing more.

Though she didn't know why,
Stella felt drawn to the apple.
So she paid the farmer for it
and brought it home
to her sisters.

Back home, the three sisters
showed each other
what they had found.

Ella and Bella didn't think
the apple was quite as exciting
as the spyglass or the horse.
But they were kind
and didn't say so.

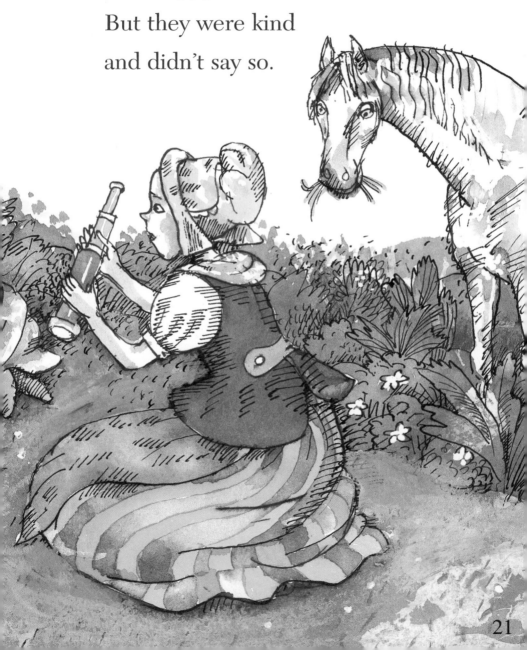

21

The next day, Ella looked
through her spyglass
and saw a distant kingdom.
In the palace lay a prince
who was gravely ill.

Doctor after doctor
had failed to cure the prince.
The queen had offered a reward.
Anyone who could save
her son's life could have
half the kingdom,
and the prince's hand in marriage.

The three sisters did not know
of the reward,
but they wanted to help the prince.

They jumped on the back
of Bella's horse.
In a flash, they were
at the prince's bedside.

"We saw the prince was ill
through my magic spyglass,"
Ella told the queen.
"We flew here on my
magic horse," said Bella.

Stella couldn't say anything.
As she looked at the dying prince,
tears filled her eyes.
She reached into her pocket
for her handkerchief
and found her apple there.

The apple seemed to glow
in Stella's hand.
"If only this could help him!"
she thought.
She cut a slice
and fed it to the prince.
He opened his eyes.

She fed him another slice.
His pale face brightened.

She fed him a third slice.
He lifted his head from the pillow
and smiled.

29

When the prince had eaten
the last bite of apple,
he got right out of bed.

He was cured!

The whole kingdom rejoiced.

"You three sisters have saved my son,"
said the queen.
"One of you may have
his hand in marriage,
and half the kingdom.
But which of you shall it be?"

The three sisters looked
at each other.
They did not want
to be unfair.
But each wanted
to marry the prince.

"Because of my magic spyglass
we saw the prince needed help,"
said Ella.

"Because of my magic horse
we got here in time," said Bella.
"Because of my magic apple
the prince is healthy once more,"
said Stella.

The queen turned to her son.
"The prince must decide,"
she said.

The prince looked at
the three sisters.
"First, there is something
I must ask each of you,"
he said.

He turned to Ella.
"Has your spyglass
been changed since you
came to my kingdom?"

Ella held her spyglass
to her eye.
She could still see
the other side of the world.
"No," she said.

The prince turned to Bella.
"Has your horse
been changed since you
came to my kingdom?"

Bella hopped on her horse
and rode him to the other side
of the world and back.
"No," she said.

The prince turned to Stella.
"Has your apple
been changed since you
came to my kingdom?"

Stella held up her apple.

All that was left was the core.

"Yes," she said with a smile.

"It has."

The prince took Stella's hand.
"Then it is you
I choose to marry," he said.
"For to help me, you gave up
something of your own.
And that is the greatest gift of all."

Ella and Bella agreed
the prince's decision was a wise one.
They were happy
for Stella's good fortune.

The prince and Stella
were married the next day.
It was a joyful wedding.
Musicians played.
Dancers danced.

And everyone in the kingdom
ate apple pie.

AUTHOR'S NOTE

The Magic Apple is based on a Jewish folktale. It illustrates the belief that to perform the best "mitzvah" (a worthy deed), you must give of yourself or give up something of your own.

The traditional story was passed down by storytellers throughout Europe and the Middle East, and is still told today. One version is Peninnah Schram's "The Magic Pomegranate," in *Jewish Stories One Generation Tells Another* (Jason Aronson, Inc., 1993).